Stories
of
Vampires

Louie Stowell

Illustrated by Gabo Bernstein

Reading consultant: Alison Kelly
Roehampton University

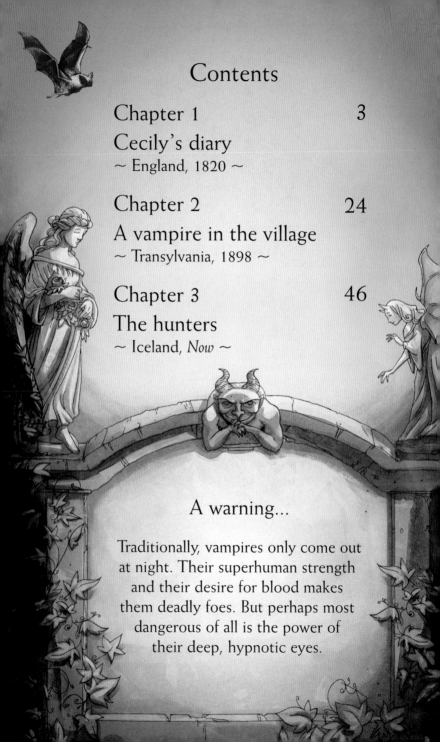

Contents

A warning...

Traditionally, vampires only come out
at night. Their superhuman strength
and their desire for blood makes
them deadly foes. But perhaps most
dangerous of all is the power of
their deep, hypnotic eyes.

Chapter 1

Cecily's diary

~ England, 1820 ~

This diary belongs to Cecily Brownswood

Saturday

I can hardly wait! Tonight is my very first ball. But last night, did I dream of waltzes, ballgowns and glittering chandeliers? Oh no. My dreams were far less pleasant...

I dreamed that my window was open and the wind was howling through. A low voice whispered, "Let me in, Cecily. Invite me in."

I heard myself say, "Come in," and a dark shape flew in through the window, like a black sheet flapping in the wind.

A moment later, a tall man in a long black cloak was in my room. His hair was jet-black and his face was very white.

He leaned forward, as though for a kiss. But I saw a glimpse of pointed teeth. They were about to sink into my neck...

As I awoke, my hand went to my neck. Of course, there was nothing there. But I've never had such a vivid dream.

Saturday night

My sisters, my parents and I crammed into the coach, headed for the ball. But I wasn't very cheerful, as my new bodice was laced up so tight that breathing was a challenge.

I wondered how on earth I was going to dance in my stiff dress, and if there'd be anyone worth dancing with. I doubted it; not in boring old Little Gidding.

I wish I lived somewhere more exciting, where I'd meet dashing officers or brave sailors or daring explorers, and be whisked away to exotic, faraway places.

The young gentlemen around here are about as exciting as cold toast.

But perhaps my luck was changing?

"I hear that someone's taken Grange Manor," said my middle sister, Charlotte, to my eldest sister, Lizzy. "Apparently he's a handsome young gentleman, though I've not seen him yet myself."

My heart began to beat a little faster at the mention of this mysterious person.

When we arrived at the dance, the party was already in full swing. A small band was playing a jaunty tune, and on one side of the room, there was a large table groaning with food and drink.

I was starving, so I started off in the

direction of the refreshments. Suddenly, among the dancing couples and milling guests, I saw a face I recognized and – I could not help it – I let out a loud, unladylike gasp. It was the pale stranger from my dream.

The next second, he was beside me. "May I have the pleasure of this dance?"

I stared at him, unable to speak.

He smiled and offered his hand to me, gazing into my eyes. Feeling dazed, I took his hand in mine. It was deathly cold.

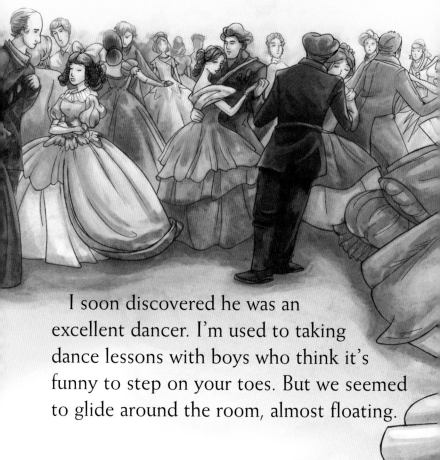

I soon discovered he was an excellent dancer. I'm used to taking dance lessons with boys who think it's funny to step on your toes. But we seemed to glide around the room, almost floating.

"Who *are* you?" I asked, partly because I wanted to know but also so he'd open his mouth and I could look at his teeth.

He didn't reply, but instead whirled me faster and faster around the dancefloor, until I was panting for air. He didn't seem to breathe faster. In fact, I couldn't hear him breathing at all.

As the song ended, my partner bowed and seemed to melt away into the crowd.

Sunday

The ball seems like just another dream today. I went to church as normal, took a walk in the fields, rode on Pebbles, and took tea with my sisters at our cousin's house nearby. But everywhere I went, I looked for the pale young man.

If he lives at the Manor, surely I'll see him soon?

Wednesday
No sign of him anywhere in town or out of it. Perhaps he'll be at Friday's ball?

Friday night
As I arrived at the ball, I saw him immediately.

My pale young man was waiting for me on the dance floor. I felt drawn towards him, like a wind-up toy, unable to control my own feet.

"You came back to me, my love," he said, as if it were the most normal way in the world to open a conversation. He took my hand and twirled me around the room. I felt as though I were in a trance.

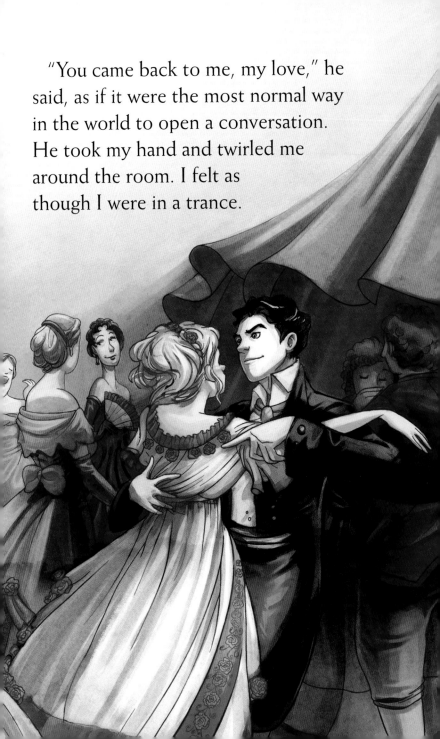

As the tune finished – I couldn't say whether it lasted minutes or hours – my partner looked at me with his deep, dark eyes. "Come into the garden," he said.

I tried to clear my head. It felt as though part of me, the sensible part, was asleep. "Only if you tell me who you are," I managed to say. "Please tell me?"

"Come," he said, "and I'll show you."

Moments later, we were on the moonlit terrace beyond the ballroom. The man's strange, beautiful face was close to mine.

His strange, beautiful, pale face... that I had never seen in daylight... with its sharp, sharp teeth... and his chest that never rose and fell to breathe...

The music indoors stopped abruptly and I was suddenly very awake. The thought that had been bubbling under the surface rose up and my heart jumped in fear as I realized... "You're a vampire!"

His face stretched into a snarl, like an animal, no longer handsome. With a terrible hiss, he lunged at me.

I ducked, and ran as fast as I had ever run. Safe inside the crowded ballroom, I turned. The vampire was nowhere to be seen.

I took a seat close to the buffet and watched and waited. To calm myself, I took a plate of food and began to pick at it. Just then, I heard a voice at my elbow. "You can't escape so easily, my love."

The vampire was standing beside me. I jerked to my feet, spilling my plate of rich, garlicky French stew everywhere. To my surprise, the vampire leaped back.

"Garlic!" he hissed, then turned and fled.

As I stared after him, I had an idea. There were wild garlic flowers growing near to my house. *As soon as I get home,* I thought, *I'll put vases of them EVERYWHERE.*

I felt much better after thinking of that.

I spent the rest of the ball dancing with a very plain boy named Tom. He had red, freckled cheeks, he breathed noisily through his mouth and he stepped on my feet, too.

That night, I thought he was the best dance partner a girl could ever want.

Chapter 2

A vampire in the village

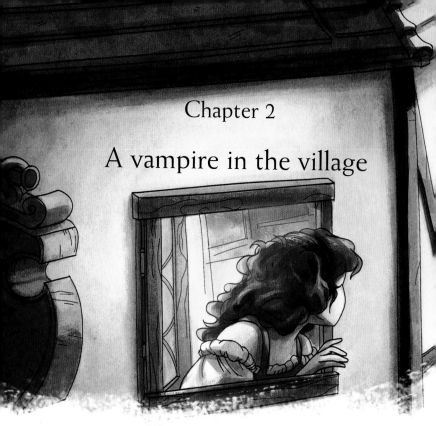

~ Transylvania, 1898 ~

The moon shone on the empty village square. Most villagers were tucked up in bed, but 16-year-old Clara was wide awake. She lived at the top of her father's noisy inn, so she rarely went to bed before midnight. It was now after one.

As the muffled singing rose up through
the floor, Clara gazed out of the window.
A shadowy figure in a black cloak was
creeping across the square. He looked like
a man, but not like any man she'd ever
seen. His skin was white as ivory, his eyes
flashed green in the dark, and his lips were
stained a ruby red.

The figure was surely moving faster than any human being could. Then, all of a sudden, he was gone.

"It must be a trick of the light," Clara thought. But, as she got into bed, her mind kept whirring. *Could it be a vampire?* "Don't be silly," she told herself. "Vampires are just an old wives' tale."

As a young girl, she'd listened eagerly as the old women of the village told tales of these creatures, and she found herself remembering snatches as she tried to sleep. *They're monsters who look like handsome men and beautiful women. They drink human blood by night. They have no reflections. A vampire leaves only two tiny wounds in his victim's neck.*

Eventually, after much tossing and turning, Clara fell asleep.

The next thing she knew, it was morning and someone was shouting.

"Dead! It's old Mr. Goga. He's dead!"

In a panic, Clara dressed as quickly as she could and ran downstairs, her skirts flying out behind her.

The whole village was pouring out into the square. Clara rushed to where the village policeman was standing, beside the lifeless body of Mr. Goga.

As Clara leaned closer, she saw two tiny puncture wounds on the old man's wrinkled neck. She shivered.

"Be off with you, Clara!" said the policeman. "This is no place for you."

Clara scurried away. What should she do? She had no doubt at all that Mr. Goga had been killed by a vampire. But who would believe her? And even if some of the older, crazier ladies of the village believed her... who'd believe *them*?

So Clara kept her suspicions to herself. Then, very late one evening, a few days later, a young man came into the inn.

He had no hat, Clara noticed, and his coat was very old. But despite his scruffy clothes, he was handsome, though pale. His eyes were bright green and his lips were far redder than a boy's usually are.

He strode up to the bar, and Clara's
father bustled over to him. "How can I
help you, sir?" he asked.

"I am looking for information about
the murder of Mr. Goga," said the young
man. His voice was quiet and serious. "I
heard he was killed a few days ago. I need
to know how."

Clara's father stared at him, suspiciously. "It's family business," the man added.

"Oh," said Clara's father, in a more sympathetic tone. "You must be a relative of the late Mr. Goga?"

Clara's father leaned forward. "I'm sorry to tell you, but his body was drained... no blood left at all, the doctor said. There were only two little wounds on the neck."

The young man nodded, as if that was what he'd expected to hear, then turned on his heel and headed for the door.

"Excuse me, Father," said Clara, grabbing her cloak and following him. "I have to go out for a while."

"Wait, where are you..." called her father, but Clara had already gone.

Outside, Clara had only taken a few paces after the young man, when he turned to face her.

"Why are you following me?" he asked.

Clara blinked, surprised that he'd heard her. But she couldn't help blurting out the question that was burning on her tongue. "Did a vampire kill Mr. Goga?"

"Yes." The boy's tone was matter-of-fact. "And I'm going to hunt him." He pulled a wooden stake from his coat, making Clara gasp.

Clara trembled at the thought of the vampire out there in the night. But she couldn't let this stranger go alone, to defend *her* village. "I'm coming with you," she said. "I'm Clara, by the way."

The boy smiled for the first time since she'd seen him. "Victor," he said.

Clara grinned too. "Do you have any more of those stakes for me?"

Victor shook his head, but pointed to the crucifix around her neck. "Use that. It will keep you safe from the vampire."

Victor led her up into the dense woods behind the village, bounding up the steep path like a mountain goat. She couldn't possibly keep up, and her lungs felt fit to burst after a few minutes.

"How... *pant*... do you... *gasp*... know... where the vampire is?" she asked him.

"I've been tracking him for a long time," said Victor. "But... stop. We're there."

In the moonlight, Clara could see the outline of a huge, stone house. They crept through the back door of the house into a long corridor, lit by torches. Victor put his finger to his lips, but the warning wasn't necessary. Clara was already creeping along like a timid mouse, jumping at every little noise.

As they reached a grand, dimly-lit hall, Clara caught sight of herself in a large mirror on the wall. Where was Victor? A surge of panic went through her and she spun around. But Victor hadn't gone anywhere. He was standing by her side... and yet he had no reflection in the mirror.

A horrible thought sprang into her mind. *Vampires have no reflection.* Then, as she looked into Victor's own bright green eyes, she remembered the green eyes of the swift-moving vampire she'd seen a few nights ago...

"You're one of them!" she cried.

Victor grabbed her arm. "Please..."

"Get off me!" Clara cried. She wriggled away, tearing her dress, and ran down the corridor... slap-bang into a figure in a long, black cloak. Freezing, vice-like hands closed around her wrists.

A horrible smile spread across his face. Up close, his skin looked so pale, it might as well have been painted white.

"I see my son has brought me a snack," he said. The vampire spun Clara around so she could see Victor, who was standing not far away. He had a dark scowl on his face, but he said nothing.

The vampire threw back his head and laughed. The sound made Clara shudder, but as he laughed, he loosened his grip. Clara saw her chance.

Pulling her hands free, she grabbed her crucifix, pressing it to the vampire's cheek. He let out a terrible, screaming hiss. Smoke billowed up from his face.

The vampire staggered back, howling, and Clara began to run. Victor lunged forward. She thought he was going to grab her, but instead, he pulled out his stake and plunged it into the vampire's chest. With a final scream, the vampire vanished in a cloud of dust.

Clara stared at Victor. "I don't understand. Why did you do that? He's your father! You're a vampire."

Victor shook his head. "Not quite," he said. "My father was." He looked at the pile of dust, a little sadly. "But my mother was human. I am what is known as a *dhampir*. I take after my father in some ways," he said. "The reflection... my strength..."

"But you didn't inherit his taste in food?" said Clara, cautiously.

Victor smiled for the second time that night. "No," he said.

They strolled out into pale morning light, arm in arm, silent for a moment.

Then Clara asked, "What next?"

"I'll continue my hunt. These mountains are crawling with vampires," said Victor. He paused. "Perhaps... you'll join me?"

"Perhaps I will," said Clara.

As they walked together down the mountainside, Clara felt excitement fizzing inside. Of course she'd join him. There was only one thing still troubling her.

How on earth, she wondered, *am I going to explain this to my father?*

Chapter 3

The hunters

~ Iceland, *Now* ~

"This is James Kim." The teacher patted James's shoulder. "Shall we welcome him to Dalvik High School, everyone?"

"Hi James," mumbled the students.

Here we go again... James thought. *Another month, another school.* His dad's job meant they were always moving.

James was fourteen years old and well-built for his age. Most people assumed he played a lot of sports. In fact, his only exercise was helping his dad at work. But since his dad, Mr. Kim, was a vampire hunter, this meant James spent most evenings running, jumping, ducking and wielding a wooden stake or a crossbow.

James glanced out of the window as the teacher waffled on through her 'be nice to the new pupil' speech. Although it was the early afternoon, it was already pitch-dark.

This place is a vampire paradise, James thought, grimly. *At this time of year, it's dark almost all the time.*

James looked around the class. *Do any of them know what's out there?* He suspected that they didn't. Hardly anyone in the world knew about vampires. James often wished that he'd never found out about them himself...

Long ago, James and his family were attacked by vampires. He and his father got away unharmed. His mother didn't get away at all. Ever since then, his father had devoted his life to killing these monsters. As soon as he was old enough, James joined him.

Dalvik was their latest stop – Mr. Kim had read about some mysterious disappearances there and was sure that vampires were responsible. They'd moved from New York to Dalvik within a week.

As James was being introduced to his new classmates, he knew his father was searching for vampire lairs.

The plan was that James and Mr. Kim would observe the creatures' movements and habits for a while, then ambush them. "But you need an education, too," his dad had insisted. So here he was.

As the teacher finished her speech, she ushered James to the only empty chair, beside a pretty girl with pale, fair hair. She smiled as he sat down.

"I'm Lara," she whispered.

James nodded hello, feeling awkward. He could fire a crossbow with pinpoint accuracy, but when it came to talking to girls, he was at a loss.

Luckily, Lara was chatty. "You're American, right? So it's a good thing it's English class first. That'll be easy for you."

"You sound fluent yourself," said James.

Lara shrugged. "I've been learning it for ages. Feels like centuries!"

James made an effort to listen to the teacher for a while, but students kept asking questions in Icelandic, so she gave up speaking English, and James's mind drifted. *I wonder where Dad is?*

He's probably underground somewhere. Mr. Kim would be searching all the sunless places in the area, from crypts and caves to cellars.

As the lesson ended, the class surged out and James found himself standing next to Lara. Her eyes glanced at his throat and she staggered back, as if she'd been stung. Then she turned and ran.

James's hand went to his neck and his fingers closed around the crucifix he wore for protection. It didn't take a genius to guess what his new 'friend' really was.

He reached into his bag, pulling out one
of the stakes he always carried with him,
then tore off after Lara, down the corridor
and out into the dark, snowy playground.

He could see Lara standing just a
short distance away in the snow. She was
shivering and shaking and looked very
weak, but that could be a trick.

"I thought your kind didn't feel the cold?" spat James, as she shivered again.

"I don't," Lara replied. "It's your crucifix. The sight of it... Please cover it?"

James shook his head. "These only hurt vamps if you touch them. You're faking." He raised his stake, but he didn't attack.

James eyed Lara cautiously. He'd stood this close to hundreds of vampires over the years. Some had pleaded with him in soft voices. But there had always been something in their eyes – something hungry and evil – that he couldn't see in Lara's open face. He found himself slipping his cross beneath his t-shirt.

Lara's shivering stopped a little.

"I don't get it," said James. "Why does just *looking* at a cross make you tremble? I've never seen a vampire do that before."

Lara looked wistful. "Hundreds of years ago, when I was your age, I was turned into a vampire. But I always craved the company of humans, so I kept coming to school. And I never wanted to hurt anyone, so I only drink animal blood. Never human. That's why I'm so weak..."

But she broke off, clearly hearing something that James couldn't.

He turned to see three figures haring towards them. A slower figure was behind them, chasing. It was James's father.

Everything seemed to happen at once. There were shouts and hisses and snarls and the sound of a crossbow being drawn back. One of the vampires leaped at James, snarling and baring his fangs.

But James's dad had trained him well. He kept calm, and raised his stake. The vampire threw itself at him, not noticing the weapon... and disappeared into dust.

"Help! Please stop! I'm on your side."

James turned in the direction of the voice – Lara's voice – to see his father raise his crossbow and point it at Lara.

Lara summoned all her strength and ran. Mr. Kim, who'd already dusted one vampire, pulled back his crossbow again...

Then James saw what Lara was running at. "Dad, look out!" he cried. A vampire in a red dress was rushing at Mr. Kim, her clawlike nails reaching for him.

Lara slammed into her. The vampire was startled for a moment, but quickly pushed Lara to the ground. "Traitor! I could snap you like a china doll. I could..."

With a **thunk**, a crossbow bolt pierced her heart.

Mr. Kim lowered his bow.

As the dust cleared, James helped Lara up. "Are you ok?" he asked.

She nodded. "I'm not THAT breakable."

Mr. Kim looked confused. "James, a vampire hunter is meant to *kill* vampires, not make friends with them."

"It's ok, she's harmless," said James.

"I'm a good vampire," Lara added.

"What are you doing out there?" A teacher was calling from the doorway.

"Not all that good, if you're skipping classes," said Mr. Kim, with a smile. "Go on!" He shooed James and Lara inside.

"Come on!" said the teacher, crossly. "You have a test in five minutes."

"Perhaps we should help my dad fight more evil undead fiends?" James muttered.

"Coward," chuckled Lara, as they went to meet their fate.

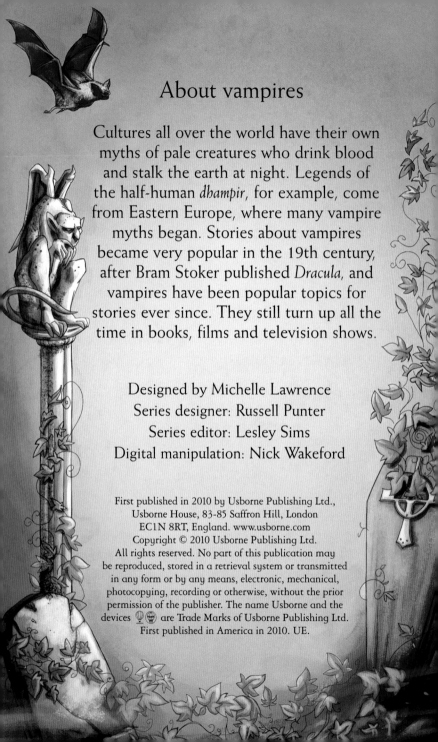

About vampires

Cultures all over the world have their own myths of pale creatures who drink blood and stalk the earth at night. Legends of the half-human *dhampir*, for example, come from Eastern Europe, where many vampire myths began. Stories about vampires became very popular in the 19th century, after Bram Stoker published *Dracula*, and vampires have been popular topics for stories ever since. They still turn up all the time in books, films and television shows.

Designed by Michelle Lawrence
Series designer: Russell Punter
Series editor: Lesley Sims
Digital manipulation: Nick Wakeford

First published in 2010 by Usborne Publishing Ltd.,
Usborne House, 83-85 Saffron Hill, London
EC1N 8RT, England. www.usborne.com
Copyright © 2010 Usborne Publishing Ltd.